This Walker book
belongs to:

....

....

....

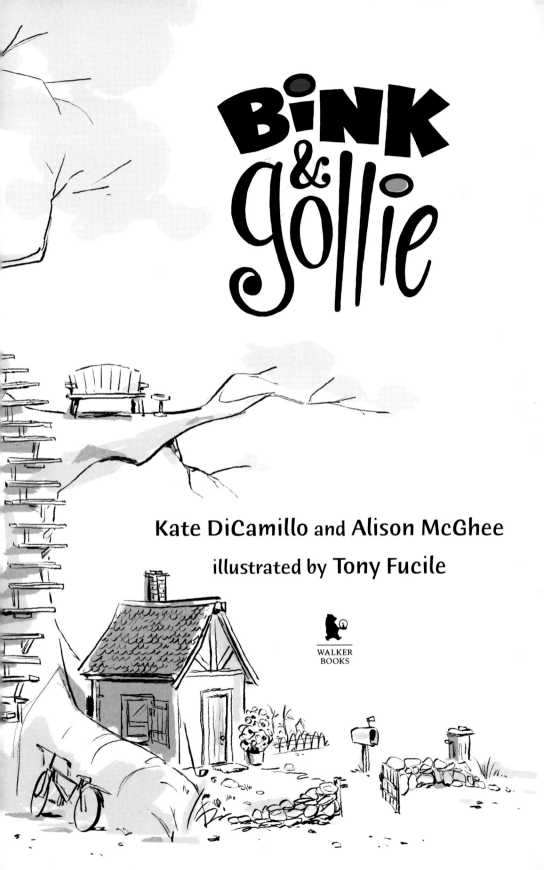

Bink & gollie

Kate DiCamillo and Alison McGhee

illustrated by Tony Fucile

WALKER
BOOKS

This is a work of fiction. Names, characters, places and incidents
either are the product of the author's imagination or, if real, are used
fictitiously. All statements, activities, stunts, descriptions, information
and material of any other kind contained herein are included for
entertainment purposes only and should not be relied on for
accuracy or replicated as they may result in injury.

First published 2010 by Walker Books Ltd
87 Vauxhall Walk, London SE11 5HJ

This edition published 2012

2 4 6 8 10 9 7 5 3 1

Text © 2010 Kate DiCamillo and Alison McGhee
Illustrations © 2010 Tony Fucile

The right of Kate DiCamillo, Alison McGhee and Tony Fucile to be identified as
authors and illustrator respectively of this work has been asserted by them
in accordance with the Copyright, Designs and Patents Act 1988

This book has been typeset in Humana Sans ITC

Printed in China

British Library Cataloguing in Publication Data:
a catalogue record for this book is available from the British Library

ISBN 978-1-4063-3901-7

www.walker.co.uk

K. D.

To Cindy Schultz Sykes, marvellous companion of my youth

A. M.

To Karen and Nina

T. F.

Contents

Don't
You
Need
a
New
Pair
of
Socks?

"Hello, Gollie," said Bink.
"What should we do today?"

"Greetings, Bink," said Gollie.
"I long for speed."

"Let's roller-skate!"

"I do need a new pair of socks!" said Bink. "Let's go inside."

"Hello," said Bink. "I'm here for the socks."

"It's a sock bonanza!" said Bink.

"Indeed it is," said Gollie. "An extremely bright sock bonanza."

"I'll take this pair," said Bink.

"Bink," said Gollie, "the brightness of those socks pains me. I beg you not to purchase them."

"I can't wait to put them on," said Bink.

"I love socks," said Bink.

"Some socks are more lovable
than others," said Gollie.

"I especially love bright socks," said Bink.

"Putting on socks is hard work," said Bink. "I'm hungry."

"Maybe Gollie is making pancakes."

"Hello, Gollie," said Bink.
"Do I smell pancakes?"
"You do not," said Gollie.
"Will I smell pancakes?"
said Bink.

"Perhaps a compromise is in order, Bink," said Gollie.

"What's a compromise?" said Bink.

"Use your grey matter, Bink," said Gollie. "You remove your outrageous socks, and I will make pancakes."

"The problem with Gollie," said Bink, "is that it's either Gollie's way or the highway."

20

"Greetings, Bink," said Gollie. "I am eating pancakes. What are you doing?"

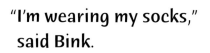
"I'm wearing my socks," said Bink.

"I have brought you half of my pancakes," said Gollie.

"And I've removed one of my outrageous socks," said Bink. "It's a compromise bonanza!"

P.S.

I'll

Be

Back

Soon

"It has been far too long since my last adventure,"
said Gollie. "I must journey forth into the wider
world. But where?
Tasmania? Timbuktu?"

"The finger has spoken," said Gollie.

"I'm baffled," said Bink.
"Am I *Whom?*"

KNOCK,
KNOCK,
KNOCK!

"I cannot talk right now," said Gollie.

"Why not?" said Bink.

"Because," said Gollie, "I am high in the
  pure air of the Andes Mountains."

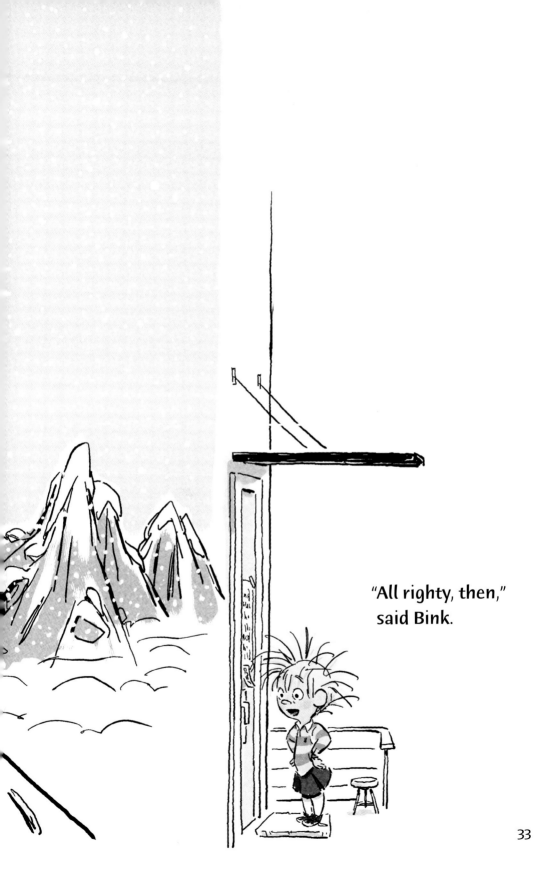

"All righty, then,"
said Bink.

33

"I wonder if Gollie's home yet," said Bink.

"Hmm," said Bink.

KNOCK,
KNOCK,
KNOCK!

"Please," said Gollie. "Have you not read the sign?"

"I've read it," said Bink. "Aren't you hungry?"

"Not at all," said Gollie.

"Not even a little?" said Bink.

"Not even a little," said Gollie.

"Not even a bit hungry?" said Bink.

"I don't believe it."

"What does *implore* mean?" said Bink.

**KNOCK,
KNOCK,
KNOCK!**

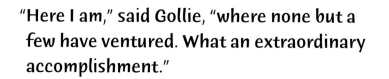

"Here I am," said Gollie, "where none but a few have ventured. What an extraordinary accomplishment."

"Bink!" said Gollie. "Come and see."

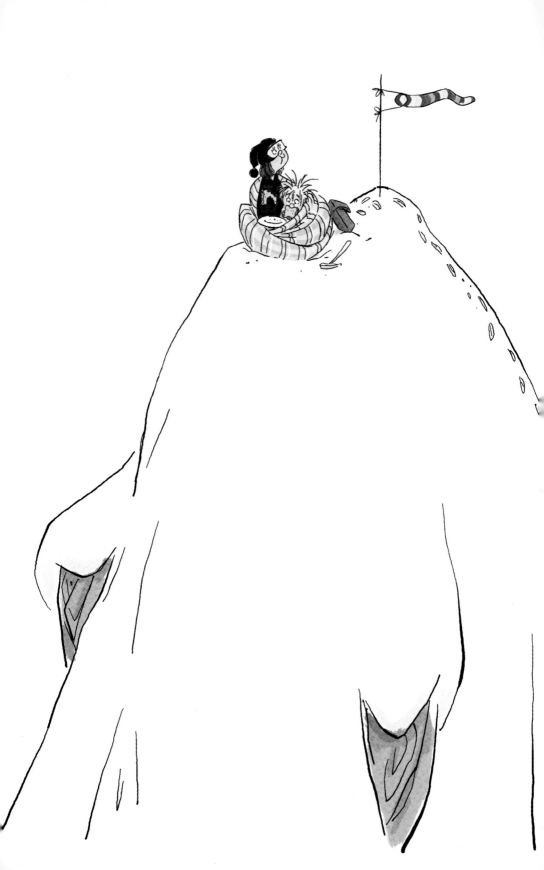

Give

a

Fish

a

Home

"As you can see," said Mr Fishman, "these are truly remarkable fish. Spectacular in virtually every way. Marvellous companions, marvellous. Each one desperate for a good home."

"I'll take that one," said Bink.

"Bink," said Gollie, "I must inform you that you are giving a home to a truly unremarkable fish."

"I love him," said Bink.

"Furthermore," said Gollie, "that fish is incapable of being a marvellous companion."

"I wonder what his name is," said Bink.

"Fred?" said Gollie.

"Yes, Fred," said Bink. "My marvellous companion."

"I've only made enough pancakes for two," said Gollie.

"Fred can share with me," said Bink.

"I only have two chairs," said Gollie.

"Oh, Fred doesn't need a chair," said Bink.

"Gollie, do you want to go and see *Mysteries of the Deep Blue Sea*?" said Bink.

"Is that the film about the fish?" said Gollie.

"It is!" said Bink. "It's the film about the fish."

"Fred thinks that was a top-quality fish film,"
  said Bink.

"I'm not sure I agree," said Gollie.

"Fred has a good idea," said Bink.

"I am almost afraid to enquire," said Gollie.

"Fred wants to roller-skate," said Bink. "Fred longs for speed."

"Fish know nothing of longing," said Gollie.

"Some fish do," said Bink. "Some fish long."

"Hey!" said Bink. "Wait
for me and Fred!"

"Don't be afraid, Fred," said Bink.

"Oh, no!" said Bink.

"HELP!"
said Bink.

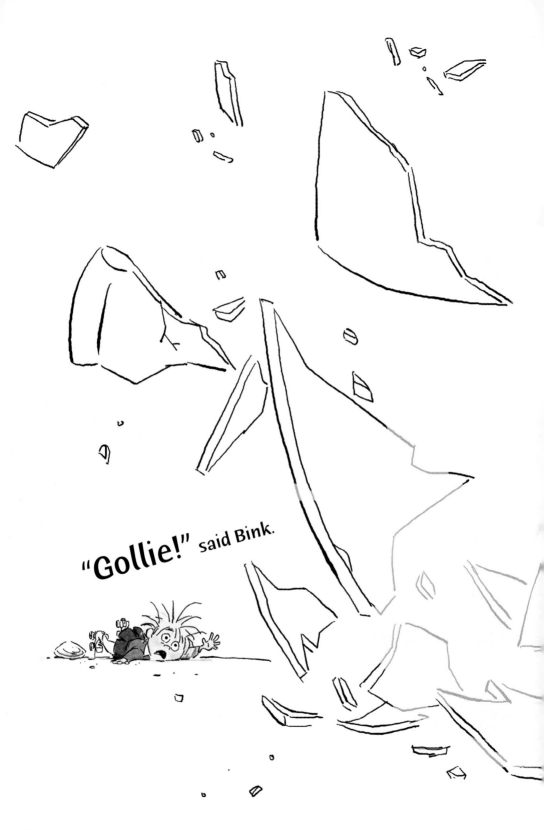

"Gollie!" said Bink.

"What are you doing?"

"Help! Give me back my fish!"

"What have you done
with Fred?" said Bink.

"I have saved Fred's life," said Gollie.

"How can Fred be my marvellous companion if he's in the pond?" said Bink.

"You can come and visit him," said Gollie. "If you feel the need for a marvellous companion."

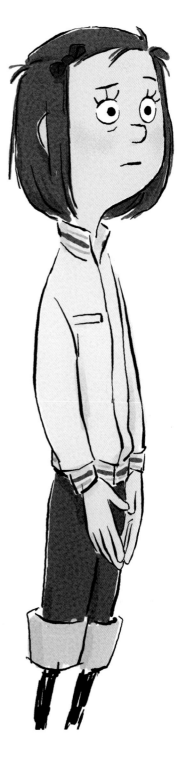

"I think you're jealous
of Fred," said Bink.

"Gollie," said Bink, "use your grey matter. Don't you know that you are the most marvellous companion of all?"

"Really?" said Gollie.

"Really," said Bink.

Six months later...

Kate DiCamillo is the author of the best-selling
The Magician's Elephant and the multiple award-winners
The Tale of Despereaux and *Because of Winn-Dixie*, and the
creator of the award-winning Mercy Watson series.
Kate DiCamillo lives in Minneapolis, USA.

Alison McGhee is the award-winning author of
The Song of Middle C; *Snap*; the number 1 bestseller *Someday*;
and the young adult novel *All Rivers Flow to the Sea*.
Alison McGhee lives in Minnesota, USA.

Tony Fucile has spent more than twenty years designing and
animating characters for cartoon feature films, including *The Lion King*
and *The Incredibles*, for which he was a supervising animator. His other
picture-book titles include *Let's Do Nothing* and *Driving to Bed*.
Tony Fucile lives in San Francisco, USA.

Look out for *Bink and Gollie: Two for One* – coming soon!

ISBN 978-1-4063-3739-6

Available from all good booksellers

www.walker.co.uk
www.binkandgollie.com